GREEN HILLS PUBLIC LIBRARY DISTRICT
S0-BEA-966

It's Time

Ada Quinlivan

illustrated by
Aurora Aguilera

New York

Published in 2017 by The Rosen Publishing Group, Inc.
29 East 21st Street, New York, NY 10010

First Edition

Managing Editor: Nathalie Beullens-Maoui
Editor: Sarah Machajewski
Book Design: Michael Flynn
Illustrator: Aurora Aguilera

Cataloging-in-Publication Data

Names: Quinlivan, Ada.
Title: Mealtime / Ada Quinlivan.
Description: New York : Powerkids Press, 2016. | Series: It's time | Includes index.
Identifiers: ISBN 9781499422801 (pbk.) | ISBN 9781499422825 (library bound) | ISBN 9781499422818 (6 pack)
Subjects: LCSH: Food–Juvenile literature. | Dinners and dining–Juvenile literature.
Classification: LCC TX355.Q85 2016 | DDC 641.3–dc23

Manufactured in the United States of America

CPSIA Compliance Information: Batch #BS16PK: For Further Information contact Rosen Publishing, New York, New York at 1-800-237-9932

Contents

I smell pancakes when I wake up.

It must be time for breakfast!

My family eats pancakes, eggs, and fruit.

We drink orange juice.

Mom says it's important to
eat breakfast.

Breakfast gives us energy for the day!

I love lunchtime at school.

We eat in the cafeteria.

My dad made my lunch.

I have a sandwich, an apple, and a cheese stick.

My friend Jamal
buys lunch.

He has spaghetti and meatballs.

I help mom make dinner after school.

We cook chicken and rice.

My sister Sara sets the table.

She puts out napkins, forks, and plates.

My family eats together
at the table.

We talk about our day.

I love mealtime.

It’s great to eat with family and friends!

Words to Know

apple

pancakes

sandwich

Index